THE FACES OF COURAGEOUS CHILDREN

Three Short Stories of Incredible Acts of Bravery

Ollie B. Wheeler III

I Am Ollie LLC
Miami, FL

ISBN 978-1-7333000-1-8

The Faces of Courageous Children tells the stories of three incredible children who overcome significant challenges to make invaluable contributions to their native lands. Dedicated to serving the greater good, these young heroes place their lives in peril to restore nations, save lives, and preserve the kingdom. The stories invite readers to be brave, no matter what they're facing.

Table of Contents

DEDICATION

To my amazingly brilliant son and godson,

I am blessed beyond words,
humbly elated,
overflowing with thanksgiving,
because of you both—
so inspired and hopeful.

Continue to live fearless lives.
Shine your lights, and
Ignite a passion in others to
be, think, and live
boldly,
selflessly,
and victoriously.

Find the courage to keep climbing to the top of the mountain, and when you have arrived, find the strength to celebrate.

A NOTE FROM THE AUTHOR

The joy of writing comes in seeing a spark of inspiration become words on a page. As both a teacher and a writer, I find great pleasure in knowing that my life and work might inspire young minds, and they might inspire me in turn. Over many years, I have had the opportunity to teach remarkable children with inspiring stories of their own—accounts of great feats, overcoming odds, and saying no to adversity. The resilience and strength of my students when faced with challenges is nothing short of extraordinary.

Their bravery prompted me to write this book.

Although the stories are completely fictional, the messages of courage and hope transcend their story-bound settings. The stories of tragedy, love, and triumph in The Faces of Courageous Children kindle deep emotions, perhaps even the ones I felt when my students shared their stories with me.

I believe that anyone can make a difference in this world. Whether your footprints are large or small, the impact you make is significant. Never be afraid to stand for what is right. Never be afraid to use your voice to affect change.

Chief among courageous acts is choosing to be yourself. In a world where everyone wants to be someone or something other than themselves, it takes great bravery to live out your purpose and be true to who you are. You do not need a cape or some magical power to be courageous. Use what you have.

True power and courage come from within.

At the end of this book, I have left space for you to tell your story. You can tell a true story or let your imagination run wild. Write your hero story and share it with your family, friends, and teachers. We should never waste a chance to inspire others!

Ollie Wheeler

THE JEWEL OF THE SEA

Uria was a beautiful island, the jewel of the sea. Every day, people traveled from far away to see Uria's dramatic landscape, enchanting sunsets, and spectacular rainbow eucalyptus trees.

In a small wooden house near the sea lived Tomás, a courageous little boy. Tomás loved drawing, playing soccer with Papá, and celebrating the big festivals that happened in Uria throughout the year.

One of Tomás's favorite festivals was El Día de la Victoria, the Day of Victory. Every year on May 19, Uria celebrated the day they won their independence from San Quisado, a larger, neighboring island. Sunup to sundown, the streets were filled with people dancing, singing, and greeting each other with kisses. Tomás loved to see the people happily singing and dancing in the streets.

But one day, life changed for Tomás.

On a dark day in mid-April, war broke out in Uria. Enemy militaries from nearby islands invaded the land.

Uria's government officials warned civilians not to wander the streets, so Tomás was stuck in his house.

As he had done every day for weeks, Tomás snuck a quick peek out the window first thing in the morning. Today, like all days since the war started, the streets were empty.

"Tomás, stop looking out that window," Mamá said in her soft but stern voice.

"But, Mamá, I want to play. What am I to do? No school. No friends. No Papá."

"Your father is keeping us safe from the bad guys."

"Mamá, I miss Papá," Tomás said.

"I do too," said Mamá.

At night, Tomás remembered Papá's stories about how he built their home with the sweat of his brow and his own two hands. Before fighting in the war, Papá worked day and night to make their spot on the island a comfortable place to live. Tomás had always admired Papá for that.

Every day to pass the time, Tomás would draw pictures of Uria, beautiful images that perfectly depicted their land.

One evening while Tomás was drawing famous buildings and monuments in Uria, he heard what sounded like fireworks. Tomás ran to the window to peek outside. But before he caught view of any brilliant lights, Mamá came rushing from the kitchen and pulled Tomás away from the window.

"Didn't I tell you to stay away from the window?" Mamá said with a compassionate yet firm whisper.

"Yes, Mamá," replied Tomás.

Mamá grabbed a throw from the couch and wrapped Tomás

in it. "Lie on the floor here," she said and then lay down next to him. Tomás could feel his mother shaking like a leaf on a tree.

The loud sounds continued into the wee hours. Some of the noises sounded far off, while others seemed right outside their front door. Late into the night, Tomás tried to peek out once more to see the fireworks. "I don't see any explosions in the sky," he said.

His mother pushed his head down. "Those aren't fireworks, Tomás," she said. "Those are gunshots. The bad men are trying to take over our land."

"Why?" Tomás asked. "Why do they want our land?"

"Our land is rich in oil, and the bad men have come to take it," Mamá explained. "Don't worry. Our land is small but has lots of heart."

"Like Papá?" Tomás asked.

"Yes, Tomás. Like Papá." Mamá smiled, and Tomás fell asleep in her arms.

The sounds of gunshots were piercing. Strange noises were heard outside of Tomás's home. The echoes of footsteps scampering around the house terrified him. But Tomás wanted to be brave. Like a lion, he leaped out of the house. "Don't destroy our land!" Tomás shouted at the bad men. "Leave now!" The evil men began to tremble with fear and fled to the ocean to escape Tomás's fury.

"Tomás, Tomás, wake up," said Mamá. Tomás was sweating, and his heart was racing.

"Do you hear that sound?" she asked.

It was morning, and for the first time in a month, the sun was piercing through the window. Sounds of joy and laughter came from outside. Tomás tiptoed over to the window and took a glimpse outside. He could not believe his eyes: his homeland, once shining and beautiful, was now dark and ruined. Still, smiles were on everyone's faces.

The war was over, and Tomás knew that Papá would restore the land in no time.

People were singing and dancing on the roads. Children were running joyfully through the dried leaves and rubble.

From far away, Tomás could see men of war returning to their families. Their faces were grimy, their clothes covered in dust. Mamá and Tomás ran outside looking for Papá.

"Hi, Mr. Sanchez. Have you seen Papá?"

"No, Tomás," responded Mr. Sanchez.

"Buenos días, Doña Teresa. ¿Has visto a mi papa?"

"No, Tomás," replied Doña Teresa.

¿Dónde está mi papa? Tomás ran throughout the neighborhood crying.

"Has anyone seen mi papa?"

"Has anyone seen my husband, Miguel Tomás García?" Mamá asked throughout the town.

There was no sign of Papá. After hours of searching the streets of Uria in distress, Mamá and Tomás tumbled to the ground and lay there crying.

The sun began to go down. The streets became empty.

"Tomás, let's go home. We will search again in the morning," said Mamá.

"But Mamá—"

"No buts, Tomás."

As Tomás walked toward home with Mamá, he kept looking back for Papá, crying out, "Papá! Papá! Papá!"

Still, there were no signs of Papá.

Once Tomás and Mamá were home, Tomás went straight to bed and pretended to fall asleep. Waiting until Mamá was fast asleep, he snuck out of the house to continue his search for Papá.

Tomás searched high and low, through the dust and debris, through the rubble and the pitch-dark.

"Papá! Papá!" yelled Tomás, as he searched and searched.

Suddenly, Tomás heard a sound from piles of rubble. A

voice. Tomás began to remove layers of debris brick by brick. With each piece removed, the voice beneath the rubble became clearer, and Tomás grew stronger.

Moments later, a man emerged from the rubble, covered in dust from the crown of his head to his feet. It was Papá.

"Papá, I missed you," said Tomás as he leaped into Papá's arms.

"I missed you too, Tomás," said Papá.

As Tomás and Papá walked home, Papá shared stories of the war and how he became trapped underneath the rubble.

"Look at our land. How will I ever rebuild?" asked Papá.

"With the sweat of your brow and your two hands. I will help you, Papá," replied Tomás.

When Tomás and Papá made it home, Mamá was awakened by the sound of their voices. She leaped out of bed and into Papá's arms.

"Mamá, why are you crying? Tomás asked. "Papá is here."

"These are happy tears, Tomás," Mamá replied.

Tomás handed Papá the beautiful artwork he drew while Papá was away at war.

"Tomás, these pictures are perfect," said Papá. "This is a blueprint for how we will rebuild our land!"

The next day, it was time to celebrate El Día de la Victoria. Mamá wore her long extravagant flowing red dress. Tomás wore the suit he always saved for church on Sundays. Papá wore his black suit, a large hat, and the polka-dot tie that Mamá bought him for his birthday. Amid the rubble and crowds of people, Mamá, Papá, and Tomás laughed, cried, sang, and danced all night long, celebrating family and their beautiful island home—Uria, the jewel of the sea.

THE SHORES OF ZONDOA

On a hot summer day in Zondoa, Agu lay in bed, thinking about his family's upcoming trip to the beach. Zondoa had the most beautiful beaches in the world. People came from all over to experience the sugar-white sands and turquoise waters. Whenever Agu was on the beach, he was at peace, without a care in the world.

Agu could no longer go to school. He used to spend most of his day in a rundown school building where he loved to read poetry, fables, and fairy tales. But one day, two government officials came to the school and announced, "This school is officially closed." For a second, Agu's heart stopped beating. According to the officials, President Obi had taken office, and he decided schools were no longer necessary, especially schools for poor people.

But at least Agu could still go to the beach. Typically, he and his family would walk three miles to the beach, but this day, Ma, Pa, baby sister Grace, and Agu took the trolley.

The streets of Zondoa were once lovely, but now there was trash, boarded-up buildings, and mangy stray dogs. Agu held his nose the whole way to block out the stench.

When they arrived at the beach, Agu sprang from the trolley, eager to get to the fun. At the entrance to the beach, however, stood a government official.

"Read the sign. Tourists and government-approved

people only," the man stated while blocking the entrance.

The poor were no longer allowed on the shores of Zondoa, a place where Agu's family had often gone. Agu stood there heartbroken and in disbelief.

The walk home was long. Ma kept patting Agu on his shoulders, telling him that things would be all right. But there was no sign of hope.

A week later, Pa was fired from his job, and the family Ma worked for had fallen on hard times—she was practically cleaning for free. Every day, Pa would go out in search of work.

"Pa, did you find a job today?" Agu would ask as soon as Pa walked through the door.

"No, son, but there's always tomorrow," Pa would respond.

One day, Pa allowed Agu to tag along. They went from business to business, only to have doors shut in their faces. The last place they visited was a restaurant. Agu could tell it was extravagant because two men dressed in fine black suits guarded the entrance.

"Get away, you bum!" one of the men yelled, shooing Pa away.

"My father is not a bum," Agu retorted. "He is a hard-working man who helped build this land."

"Let's go home, Agu," Pa said with a smile on his face and his head held high. "There's always tomorrow."

Pa could not find a job, so he worked as many odd jobs as he could find to take care of the family.

Four years later, Agu still had not returned to school. He began to miss school almost as much as he missed the ocean. He yearned to read a good book near the shores, with his toes in the sand and the breeze softly touching his back.

Life in Zondoa was becoming more and more difficult. There were no jobs. The streets were filled with drifters. Bartering became the way of life until people ran out of items to exchange. There was a shortage of food, and the government snubbed those in need. If Agu had one meal a day, he was lucky. Agu never imagined that life would be so hard.

Then one hot summer day in June, Ma became ill. After several visits to the hospital, they found out Ma would need surgery. Pa was forced to enlist in Zondoa's military to pay for Ma's treatment.

But at least they had food again. Every day, the government would send them food labeled "For military families only." You could be put in prison if you shared meals with anyone who was not a family member of a military person. Agu saved and collected leftovers from other military families in his neighborhood and hid the food in the basement of his home.

Then a civil war broke out. A significant part of the

population began to fight and openly rebel against the corrupt government. No one could visit or travel to or from the country. The beaches of Zondoa were left abandoned.

Agu spent his days taking care of Ma, who was recovering from her surgery, and his sister Grace. Despite the restriction on sharing food and visiting the beach, Agu met with women and children on the shores of Zondoa at night and fed them whatever food he had. The beaches became their sanctuary. During the day, the people would hide in the mountains to await Agu's arrival at the beach with his wagon loaded with food.

But the war got worse, and the government stopped providing food to military families. Many people grew ill and died.

One night, Agu made his way to the beaches with what little food he had but was spotted by government officials. As soon as Agu began to pass out the last of his food, the officials closed in, and the people of Zondoa scattered to the mountains.

"We are citizens of Zondoa," Agu proclaimed. "These shores belong to the people. Our ancestors fought so that we could have rights to this land."

The officials did not listen and rounded up Agu and many of the women and children. They were taken to a camp where thousands of others were held.

When Pa got word that Agu was arrested for feeding

nonmilitary families, he petitioned President Obi for Agu's release. When President Obi denied Pa's request, Pa, outraged, began to quietly gather men to fight against the government.

While Pa worked to overthrow the government, Agu lived among the children, women, and men imprisoned in the camp. Many were underfed and ill, so Agu found favor with several soldiers, who secretly worked with him to nurse the sick back to health. The soldiers snuck food, medicine, and books into the camp, which Agu distributed to those in need. At night, he read to them and shared words of hope, offering the people the same peace he felt while reading on the shores of Zondoa.

When President Obi learned that most of the military was plotting against him, he and his men tried to flee the country, but they were arrested. They were found with stolen money—millions of unpaid dollars that belonged to the citizens. Once word traveled throughout Zondoa that President Obi was captured, the war ended.

Agu and the prisoners were freed from the camp. Some of them were afraid and had nowhere to go. The land was devastated, but at least they were free.

Ma, Pa, and Grace were there to greet Agu, who was happy to see his family but saddened by the devastation of the land. He wanted to be near the beaches and hear the waves softly beating against the shore. Agu feared that the beaches he so deeply loved were destroyed forever. He could think of only one thing to help his country.

"Ma. Pa. I want to be President," Agu declared.

Ma smiled. "You would be a wonderful president, but are you sure you want to take on such a burden at such a young age?"

"Yes, Ma. I have never been as sure about anything in my life," replied Agu. "I know that some people may despise my youth, but I will show them that I am ready to lead this country into better days."

"That sounds great, son" Pa responded. "My son will be the next president of Zondoa!"

The elections were less than three months away. Agu, Ma, Pa, and Grace made signs with the paper they found around the house. They put up signs on every corner and every standing building. People came from all over Zondoa to lend their support. Pa helped Agu gain the support of the military.

Agu traveled to every city, every village, and town, not only to encourage people to vote for him but to promise that life would get better. With kisses and handshakes, the people celebrated Agu, and the smiles on their faces warmed Agu's heart.

Even up to election day, Agu regularly visited the ocean. He cleaned the beaches until the sugar-white sands were free of litter and debris. The beach's ability to survive under tough circumstances reminded Agu of the strength and courage he would need if he was to become the next president.

As Agu was standing on the shore, a rainbow appeared. News traveled throughout the land that Agu had become the newly elected President of Zondoa.

Amid the crowd of people gathered along the seashore, Agu vowed to restore dignity and equality and to rebuild the land.

"Today, most of our land remains in waste, but tomorrow we will rebuild. Tomorrow our country will rejoice a little louder, stand a little taller, and shine a little brighter. If all is not accomplished, with courage and strength we will say, 'There's always tomorrow.'"

The people began to cheer. There was hope, and it echoed from the shores of Zondoa throughout the land.

KALISSA'S DIAMOND

For many years, King Noah ruled Plutonamus, a small, beautiful, and prosperous country surrounded by breathtaking, crystal-clear waters, jade-green fields, and gentle mountains that overlooked the land. Then, one day, King Noah's army rebelled against him and seized control of the kingdom.

Several years before King Noah lost his kingdom, his wife died, and he was left on his own to raise Princess Kalissa, his brave and boisterous daughter. Princess Kalissa was the apple of his eye. He cherished her above all, including his most treasured possession, the red diamond. The diamond had been passed down through the royal family from one generation to the next. King Noah couldn't wait for the day when he would hand the diamond to his daughter.

When King Noah ruled Plutonamus, he cared about the people of his kingdom, and he did all he could to help them live happy lives. He fed the poor and took care of the widows and orphans. As a result, the people thought of him as a kind leader.

But one person secretly despised King Noah.

Xerticus, the king's younger brother, was Plutonamus's military leader and right hand to King Noah. But Xerticus was jealous of his brother, and it was he who convinced the military that the king was too weak to lead the country.

"King Noah will circumvent war at any cost," Xerticus ranted. "We cannot have a leader who makes friends with our enemies. His poor and cowardly leadership will be the downfall of our nation."

One afternoon, while the king and his daughter sat on the royal throne, the king's troops approached them and demanded that King Noah release all power to his brother, Xerticus. The king was stunned.

"This is madness!" yelled the king. "How dare you approach my throne with this folly?"

"You imbeciles! My father is your king," Princess Kalissa shouted.

"Neither my power nor my kingdom can be stripped away. Take cover, my dear Kalissa. Guards, approach the throne!"

Immediately, the royal guards who were looking on raised their swords against the traitorous troops.

Princess Kalissa ran out of harm's way as her father had instructed. The king grabbed his sword from behind the throne and fought alongside his men.

One by one, the royal guards fell. Facing an overwhelming force with their swords outstretched, the king stood alone.

"Do not lay a sword to him," said Xerticus, eyeing the king. "He is useless. Brother, you are officially banished from the palace. All rights to the kingdom now belong to me, the rightful heir to the throne. Now, bow before your king."

In times past, King Noah had singlehandedly fought and defeated many great armies—he conquered territories and usurped wicked kings. His daring heart and fiery spirit would not allow him to bow to Xerticus.

Meanwhile, Princess Kalissa crept into the chambers where gold, silver coins, and Plutonamus's most precious red diamond were kept. She gathered up the diamond and a bag of coins and hid them in her trousers. Although she knew her father wanted her to escape, her heart compelled her to return to his side.

"Are you okay, father," Princess Kalissa asked.

The king nodded.

Xerticus directed his soldiers to escort the former king and princess out of the palace.

"You will never get away with this," Princess Kalissa declared.

Xerticus only grinned.

The king and his daughter were carried in a horse and buggy many miles outside the royal gates to a small wooden house.

"Father, you are bleeding," said Princess Kalissa.

"Why did you come back?" King Noah asked in a faint voice.

"I couldn't leave you. As the princess, it is my solemn duty to help protect the throne and not cower in the face of evil. This is what you taught me, father."

"This is true, my dearest Kalissa. But you are my only child, a miracle in my old age. My heart would fail if anything were to happen to you," explained King Noah. "You must always choose wisdom over emotions."

Princess Kalissa cleaned and wrapped her father's wounds and made sure he was comfortable. Right before sunset, she went out to catch fish at the lake. With her bare hands, she caught two medium-sized fish and prepared them for supper. But the king did not eat much.

After three days of rest, King Noah recovered and wrapped himself in sackcloth and ashes to mourn the loss of his kingdom.

Princess Kalissa could not bear to see her father so sad. "Father, will you eat? I will make the stew like Mom use to make, just how you like it," said the princess. "I will go to the market and handpick the finest vegetables, herbs and spices, and a fatted calf."

"We don't have any money for these things," stated the king. "And what will the people say when they see their beloved princess in the market?"

"Father, give no thought to trivial matters. Doth the fowls of the air eat? Surely the king and his daughter shall feast."

Princess Kalissa kissed her father and set out for the market.

Once Xerticus discovered that the red diamond was missing, he shouted insults and threats at his servants, turned the palace upside down, and issued harsh decrees throughout the land. More than his desire to be king, Xerticus wanted riches. The diamond made Plutonamus the wealthiest country in the Middle East, and without the diamond, the country would be deemed insignificant.

When Xerticus concluded that the diamond was taken by the former royals, he sent his men out to fetch the diamond from the banished king and princess. The men charged through King Noah's home and demanded that he return the diamond. King Noah was baffled, still unaware that his daughter had taken the diamond. The men ransacked the house in a desperate search but failed to recover the diamond.

Just as the men prepared to haul away the king, Princess Kalissa returned from the market. She instantly recognized the malicious men from the night she and her father were ejected from the palace, so she hid and watched from behind the tall bushes by the house.

The men taunted and roughly handled the king before carting him away. Princess Kalissa was distraught and questioned her decision to hide, but she knew there was not much she could do if the men took her prisoner. Still, she wanted to be with her father.

King Noah was brought before Xerticus.

"Where is the diamond, and where is that unruly daughter of

yours?" Xerticus asked.

King Noah refused to speak.

"I want everyone in all of Plutonamus to know that if I do not have the diamond by the end of the week, this mute will be lunch for the lions. Lock him away."

When news traveled throughout the country that King Noah was imprisoned, and Xerticus had become king, the people were outraged. Day and night, large crowds protested for King Noah's release. A small group of widows and orphans demanded help and begged for food, water, and other necessities. Xerticus ignored their demands and sent them away empty-handed and dismayed.

The crowd returned the next day, and then the next. But over time, the military became violent with the people, and the crowd began to dwindle until there were no protestors or beggars outside of the palace. The country was in turmoil; the people had to fend for themselves. Xerticus did not care that the people suffered. He refused to send monetary aid to the needy citizens and the developing countries that King Noah supported.

Princess Kalissa traveled to Colgea by boat, a three-day journey. The princess pleaded for help from King Jaffa, the ruler of Colgea, a large, powerful country and ally to Plutonamus. King Jaffa and King Noah were great friends.

"My father has been imprisoned, and his kingdom has been

unlawfully stripped from him. It will take the power of your nation to help restore the land," cried Princess Kalissa. "The people of Plutonamus are suffering. Your country and other countries will suffer too under the rule of my uncle."

"I am sorry, Princess Kalissa, but I wish not to get involved in family affairs," stated King Jaffa.

Princess Kalissa was desperate. She wanted her father and his kingdom back, so she offered to give King Jaffa the red diamond in exchange for his support. This would make Colgea the most powerful and wealthiest nation in the Middle East.

"Although your offer is very enticing," said King Jaffa, "I would have to gather my men for the three-day journey. This would leave my country vulnerable to threats. The risk would be too great. Still, it would be ill-advised to say yea or nay at this time."

Princess Kalissa felt discouraged by King Jaffa's refusal to give a definitive answer. She knew that if she wanted to see her father alive again, she had to move quickly and devise an alternative plan to free him.

No one knew the palace better than the princess. Remembering a secret entrance in and out of the palace, the princess knew that if she could get past the guards stationed outside the courts, she would be able to enter the palace to search for her father. Princess Kalissa drew a map of the palace and devised a plan to rescue the king before setting out.

In the middle of the night, Princess Kalissa took a path through the woods that led to the secret palace entrance. She was careful to go unseen, as she had done many times before when sneaking back into the palace after playing with the commoners by the lake.

The palace was dark. The only light was the flickering of candles. Princess Kalissa needed to make her way to the larder by the kitchen that led to a tunnel, an underground passage. The first royal family used the tunnel to escape harm during the War of 1510. After the war, some areas of the palace had to be rebuilt. The tunnel, now concealed by the floor's wooden planks, provided access to several rooms, including the one that Princess Kalissa thought would hold King Noah. In other treacherous times, spies and dangerous men were locked in this room.

Princess Kalissa tiptoed her way through the palace. Quiet as a mouse, she snuck into the larder and made her way to the small room on the other side of the palace. Princess Kalissa slowly peeked her head into the room, lifting up a wooden plank in the floor. She could see her father lying on a small cot and hear the guards outside of the tiny room. Not wanting to startle her father or be seen by the guards, she softly whispered. "Father?"

King Noah was surprised to hear his daughter's voice. "What are you doing here?" he asked.

"I am here to rescue you," replied Princess Kalissa. "Come on, Dad. Let's go."

When the guards noticed the king was not in the room, they sounded the alarm in search of the king. Princess Kalissa and King Noah could hear the warnings and hastened footsteps outside the tunnel. They had to be brave and move quickly to escape. They were halfway to the exit.

"Come on, Dad. We're almost there."

The king looked frail. Although weary from his captivity, he mustered the strength to continue on the escape route.

"I am so proud of you, Kalissa," said King Noah. "You have the beauty of your mother and the courage of King David."

"Father, my bravery comes from you. You have slayed many great giants, but what I admire most is your courage to rule the people with love and kindness," said Princess Kalissa. "We're a few steps away."

As they exited the tunnel, they found themselves surrounded by Xerticus's men. A messenger sent word to Xerticus that the exiles had been seized. Xerticus demanded that King Noah and Princess Kalissa immediately appear before his throne.

"Do you have my diamond?" asked Xerticus.

"As I told you before, we do not have the diamond," said King Noah.

"Prepare the lion's den," ordered Xerticus.

Immediately, Princess Kalissa spoke. "Father, I have the diamond."

Surprise washed over King Noah's face.

Xerticus grinned hungrily. "Give me the diamond, defiant little girl."

A soldier approached Princess Kalissa, and she reluctantly handed the diamond over.

"Tonight, my dear brother, you will be executed in front of the entire nation. As for you, my niece, you will be a vagrant in the streets of Plutonamus," declared Xerticus. "For now, take them away and place them in shackles."

Just as the guards were getting ready to take them away, King Jaffa and a grand company of his finest warriors invaded the palace.

King Jaffa demanded, "Xerticus, release the king and his daughter, and hand over that diamond."

"I will do no such thing," said Xerticus.

"Do you wish to die in battle today? I have over two thousand men with me, and you have three hundred," said King Jaffa. "What are the odds you'll still be standing after I release this great fury on you and your men?"

Xerticus commanded his men to fight, but they trembled in fear and instead released King Noah and Princess Kalissa.

"You cowards! How dare you defy my authority!" shouted Xerticus.

King Jaffa ordered his soldiers to round up Xerticus's men. Xerticus tried to escape but was immediately apprehended. Princess Kalissa charged over to Xerticus and stripped the diamond from his hand.

"King Jaffa, this belongs to you, as promised."

"Thank you, Princess Kalissa, but this diamond must remain in Plutonamus. As an ally and friend to your father, our country is bonded in peace and unity. We are committed to the welfare of your people, and we are bound to oppose all threats to either of our countries without recompense."

Princess Kalissa smiled and humbly bowed before King Jaffa. She then handed the diamond to her father. As soon as King Noah took hold of the diamond, his regal demeanor and strength returned. The king thanked King Jaffa and then hugged his daughter.

"Princess Kalissa, your name means 'great joy.' You will bring this country great joy as you sit on the throne and reign as queen of Plutonamus," the king announced. "This diamond belongs to you, my bold and courageous daughter. Kalissa's diamond will remain in Plutonamus for all of eternity, and our land shall forever be prosperous. All hail our great queen!"

Princess Kalissa was surprised—so surprised that words failed her for a moment.

"You have shown the bravery of a thousand well-prepared men for battle. Your integrity, courage, and ability to make prudent decisions will make you a great queen." King Noah declared. "I turn over my reigns because you, my fearless daughter, have consistently demonstrated that you are ready to lead this nation."

With humility, Princess Kalissa sat on the throne and delivered her first decree as queen, "Today I have decided to side with mercy. Xerticus, my father's brother, you will be banished not only from this palace but from this country. You and your men will live out your days as prisoners in foreign lands. As the queen of Plutonamus, I will rule with love, kindness, and courage—as my father taught me."

The next day, as the news traveled throughout Plutonamus that Princess Kalissa had become queen, the people gathered in front of the royal palace. They sang and danced, rejoiced, and chanted, "All hail the queen! All hail, Queen Kalissa!"

Write your Hero Story here.

(Title)

_____

_____

_____

_____

_____

_____

_____

_____

_____

_____

_____

_____

_____

_____

_____

_____

_____

_____

_____

_____

_____

_____

_____

I will face my fears and overcome them.

I will be courageous despite the presence of fear.

I will find the courage to never give up.

I will have the courage to pursue my dreams.

_____

_____

_____

_____

_____

_____

_____

_____

_____

_____

_____

_____

_____

_____

_____

_____

_____

_____

_____

_____

_____

_____

I am strong, bold, and courageous.

_____

_____

_____

_____

_____

_____

_____

_____

_____

_____

_____

_____

_____

_____

_____

_____

_____

_____

_____

_____

_____

_____

_____

I am fearless and powerful.

_____

_____

_____

_____

_____

_____

_____

_____

_____

_____

_____

_____

_____

_____

_____

_____

_____

_____

_____

_____

_____

_____

I have the courage to stand for what is right.

_____

_____

_____

_____

_____

_____

_____

_____

_____

_____

_____

_____

_____

_____

_____

_____

_____

_____

_____

_____

_____

_____

I have the courage to be me.

_____

_____

_____

_____

_____

_____

_____

_____

_____

_____

_____

_____

_____

_____

_____

_____

_____

_____

_____

_____

_____

_____

_____

_____

Fear will never rob me of success.

_____

_____

_____

_____

_____

_____

_____

_____

_____

_____

_____

_____

_____

_____

_____

_____

_____

_____

_____

_____

_____

_____

I have the courage to succeed.

I am equipped to make courageous choices.

_____

_____

_____

_____

_____

_____

_____

_____

_____

_____

_____

_____

_____

_____

_____

_____

_____

_____

_____

_____

_____

I will dream big and live courageously.

_____

_____

_____

_____

_____

_____

_____

_____

_____

_____

_____

_____

_____

_____

_____

_____

_____

_____

_____

_____

_____

_____

I believe that tomorrow will be better, so today, I take courage.

_____

_____

_____

_____

_____

_____

_____

_____

_____

_____

_____

_____

_____

_____

_____

_____

_____

_____

_____

_____

_____

_____

The brave me will show up today.

I will positively impact the world.

_____

_____

_____

_____

_____

_____

_____

_____

_____

_____

_____

_____

_____

_____

_____

_____

_____

_____

_____

_____

_____

I will courageously tell my story.

And I will live out my wildest dreams.